Dear Parent:
Your child's love of reading starts here!

Every child learns to read in a different way and at his or her own speed. Some go back and forth between reading levels and read favorite books again and again. Others read through each level in order. You can help your young reader improve and become more confident by encouraging his or her own interests and abilities. From books your child reads with you to the first books he or she reads alone, there are I Can Read Books for every stage of reading:

SHARED READING
Basic language, word repetition, and whimsical illustrations, ideal for sharing with your emergent reader

BEGINNING READING
Short sentences, familiar words, and simple concepts for children eager to read on their own

READING WITH HELP
Engaging stories, longer sentences, and language play for developing readers

READING ALONE
Complex plots, challenging vocabulary, and high-interest topics for the independent reader

ADVANCED READING
Short paragraphs, chapters, and exciting themes for the perfect bridge to chapter books

I Can Read Books have introduced children to the joy of reading since 1957. Featuring award-winning authors and illustrators and a fabulous cast of beloved characters, I Can Read Books set the standard for beginning readers.

A lifetime of discovery begins with the magical words "I Can Read!"

Visit www.icanread.com for information
on enriching your child's reading experience.

For Collin
—L.M.S.

For Alex
—S.K.H.

ISBN 978-0-545-41530-9

12 11   14 15 16/0

Printed in the U.S.A.   40

First Scholastic printing, October 2011

I Can Read!

SHARED
My First
READING

Happy Halloween, Mittens

story by **Lola M. Schaefer**

pictures by **Susan Kathleen Hartung**

SCHOLASTIC INC.
New York Toronto London Auckland
Sydney Mexico City New Delhi Hong Kong

Nick is getting ready
for Halloween.
Mittens wants to help.

Nick paints spooky faces.

Mittens paints faces, too.

"Oh, Mittens," says Nick.
"You are not helping!"

Nick puts up
a spooky cobweb.

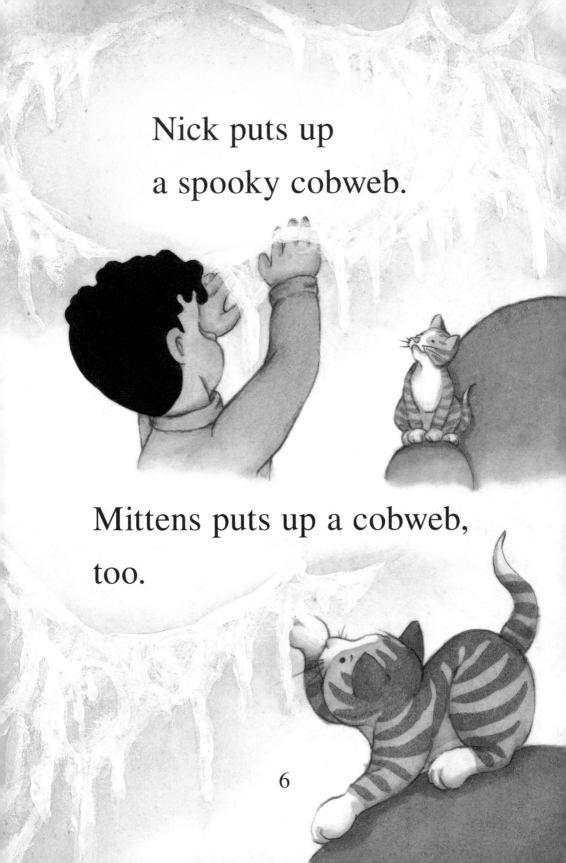

Mittens puts up a cobweb,
too.

Oops!

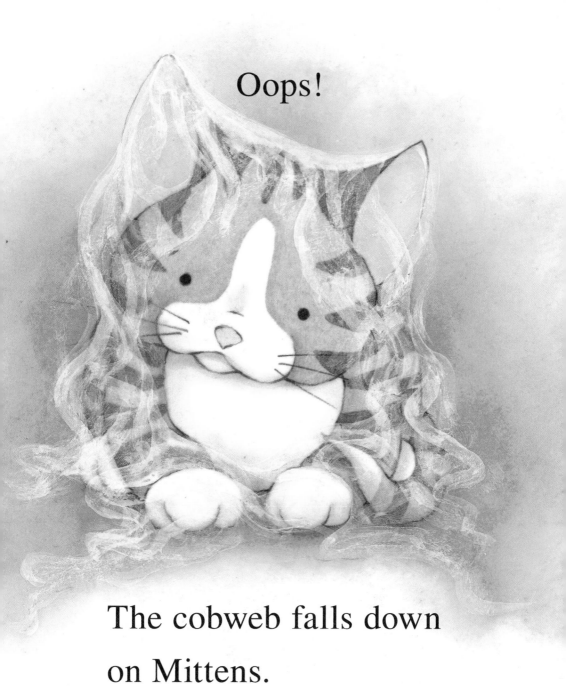

The cobweb falls down
on Mittens.

"Oh, Mittens," says Nick.
"You are not helping!"

Nick makes spooky cookies.

Mittens makes cookies, too.

"Oh, Mittens," says Nick.
"You are not helping at all!"

Mittens runs away.

Mittens licks

and licks

and licks.

13

Soon, he is clean and fluffy.

Mittens still wants to help.

Mittens finds Nick
on the porch.

Nick hangs a ghost.

The ghost blows in the wind.

"This ghost is not spooky,"
says Nick.
"I don't know what to do!"

Nick watches the ghost.

Mittens watches the ghost, too.

He jumps up.

The ghost blows past Mittens.

19

Mittens bats the ghost.
Scratch!

Mittens bats the ghost again.
Scratch!

Mittens moves away.
A spooky ghost blows
in the wind.

"Thank you for helping,
Mittens," says Nick.
"Now we are ready
for Halloween!"

Boo!

Meow!